SPY TOYS

MARK POWERS

illustrated by Tim Wesson

BLOOMSBURY

NEW YORK LONDON OXFORD NEW DELHI SYDNEY

First published in Great Britain in January 2017
by Bloomsbury Publishing Plc
Published in the United States of America in January 2018
by Bloomsbury Children's Books
www.bloomsbury.com

Bloomsbury is a registered trademark of Bloomsbury Publishing Plc

For information about permission to reproduce selections from this book, write to
Permissions, Bloomsbury Children's Books, 1385 Broadway, New York, New York 10018
Bloomsbury books may be purchased for business or promotional use. For information on
bulk purchases please contact Macmillan Corporate and Premium Sales Department at
specialmarkets@macmillan.com

Library of Congress Cataloging-in-Publication Data
Names: Powers, Mark (Comics author) | Wesson, Tim, illustrator.
Title: Spy toys / by Mark Powers ; illustrated by Tim Wesson.
Description: New York : Bloomsbury, 2018.
Summary: Three toys with tiny computerized brains, rejected because they are
not good with children, are recruited by Auntie Roz to be spy toys, whose first mission
is to save a senator's son from being kidnapped.
Identifiers: LCCN 2017022131 (print) • LCCN 2017037960 (e-book)
ISBN 978-1-68119-665-7 (hardcover) • ISBN 978-1-68119-710-4 (e-book)
Subjects: | CYAC: Toys—Fiction. | Spies—Fiction. | Kidnapping—Fiction. |
Presidents—Family—Fiction.
Classification: LCC PZ7.1.P695 Spy 2018 (print) | LCC PZ7.1.P695 (e-book) |
DDC [Fic]—dc23
LC record available at https://lccn.loc.gov/2017022131

Typeset by Westchester Publishing Services
Printed and bound in the U.S.A. by Berryville Graphics Inc., Berryville, Virginia
2 4 6 8 10 9 7 5 3 1

All papers used by Bloomsbury Publishing, Inc., are natural, recyclable products
made from wood grown in well-managed forests. The manufacturing processes
conform to the environmental regulations of the country of origin.

For Hugo, Caitlin, Lissa & Cai

With thanks to Kate, Zöe, Hannah,
Ian, Katie, Tim & Jo

CHAPTER ONE
IF HUGS COULD KILL

It was a normal Tuesday morning at the factory of Snaztacular Ultrafun, the world's biggest toy manufacturer. Hundreds of conveyor belts whirred and clanked, carrying thousands of gleaming new toys toward the brightly colored boxes in which they would be packed and delivered to shops. Balls, bikes, building blocks . . . dolls, dominoes, ducks . . . whistles, walkie-talkies, water pistols—the factory made them all.

Snaztacular Ultrafun's toys were not like the ones made by other companies. They were much cleverer and much more fun. Every toy contained a tiny computerized brain that gave it a personality and allowed it to walk and talk as if it were alive. They were the ultimate playthings: bikes that took you home if you were too tired to pedal, soccer balls that wanted to be kicked, board games whose pieces tidied themselves away once you had finished playing with them, dolls that acted just like real people. Children went crazy over them.

A red light flashed on a control panel. An alarm hooted.

"Yikes!" cried a white-coated technician who had been monitoring that morning's toy production, leaping out of his chair in surprise and banging his knee on the leg of his desk.

As each toy trundled on its way along the conveyor belt, it underwent a complicated series of scans and tests to make sure it was working properly. The company was rightly proud of its products, and it wanted each toy to be perfect for the child who would eventually play with it. The red light meant a fault had been detected in one of the toys. And if the technician let a faulty toy leave the factory, he would get in big trouble with his boss.

Rubbing his knee, the technician examined his computer screen. The system had detected a problem with one of the Snugaliffic Cuddlestar teddy bears. The Snugaliffic Cuddlestar line of teddy bears was the most advanced money could buy. The bears could sing lullabies, tell bedtime stories, bring you a glass of warm milk—but most of all they were designed for cuddling. When you hugged one of these bears, it actually hugged you back. In a world where many parents were simply too busy to do trivial things like hug their children, the teddy bears sold in their millions.

The technician jabbed a button on his control panel. A huge metal claw descended from the ceiling and snatched the faulty teddy bear from the conveyor belt.

★ ★ ★

The teddy bear's eyes flickered open. He had been expecting to find himself in a cardboard box, rattling along the road in the back of a truck on his way to a toy store. Instead, he saw that he was in a dingy metal room. There was a table, a chair, a computer, a half-eaten ham sandwich. But no children to play with. He frowned. What was going on?

The door opened and the white-coated technician entered. He was carrying a large

object that was hidden under
a white sheet. He placed the object on the
floor and consulted his computer screen.

"You are Snugaliffic Cuddlestar serial
number 427935, yes? Made this morning?"

The teddy bear nodded. "Yep."

"It says here you've been assigned the name Dan. Is that correct?"

"That's me," said the teddy bear. All Snaztacular Ultrafun toys were given individual names to help make them unique.

"Well, Dan, it's like this. The computer says you're faulty, and it's up to me to find out whether it's something that can be fixed. We have a reputation for making the best toys in the world, and we can't let shoddy merchandise out into the market, can we?"

"Whatever you say, pal," said Dan the teddy bear. He wasn't interested in boring stuff about markets or companies' reputations. He was programmed for fun.

"Good," said the technician. "Let's get started." He whipped the sheet off the mysterious object he had brought with him.

Dan's large brown eyes widened in surprise. The object appeared to be a little girl with a miserable expression and outstretched arms. She looked in serious need of a hug.

The technician rapped his knuckles on the girl's head. It made a hollow metallic sound. "This is a hug test dummy," he explained. "The electronics inside it will tell us how good you are at hugging. Pressure, duration, snuggliness, and so forth. Kindly hug the dummy for me, Dan."

Dan dashed forward. This was more like it! He was made for hugging, and now he had a chance to do some! He embraced the dummy girl in his furry arms and gave her a good squeeze.

There was a screech of wrenching metal followed by a loud bang. Dan stepped back, shocked. The dummy girl fell to the floor, her back bent horribly out of shape, her arms twisted at alarming angles and smoke pouring gently from her ears.

The technician raised his eyebrows. *"Oh dear."*

"What happened?" asked Dan.

The technician waved a small electronic device over Dan's head. The device bleeped, and the technician consulted a little screen set into it. "Ah. Just as I thought. Unfortunate."

"What is it?"

"You have a faulty snuggle chip. It's telling

8

your robotic limbs to use a thousand times the usual pressure. In simple terms, you don't know your own strength. I'm afraid you can't be allowed near children." He gestured to the twisted remains of the hug test dummy. "Imagine if you did that to a real child. That would *not* be good for business."

Dan shrugged. "So reprogram me. Make me less strong."

The technician shook his head. "Much too fiddly to reprogram a single microchip. More trouble than it's worth, I'm afraid. Far easier to take you apart and start from scratch."

"Take me *apart*?" Dan's robotic heart suddenly thumped with fear.

"Don't worry," said the technician with a sickly smile. "It won't hurt. Well, not much." He pointed to a large yellow *X* painted on the floor of the room. "Kindly stand on the *X* for me, Dan, if you would."

Dan shuffled over to the *X*. His furry brows knitted in confusion. "Why here?"

"Because that's where the trapdoor is."

CHAPTER TWO

DOLL EAT DOLL

Dan found himself tumbling down a dark metal chute. He bumped and rattled against its sides for a short time until finally it spat him out onto a cold stone floor. He stood up, brushing the dust from his fur.

He was in an enormous darkened room. The floor was littered with old bits of cardboard, cogs, springs, and broken pieces of electronic circuitry. Strange, indistinct shapes were moving all around him. The air was filled with a sickly mechanical humming sound.

"Hello?" he called nervously. This didn't

seem like a happy place. There were probably people around who could do with a nice big hug, he thought. Then he realized what might happen if he *did* hug someone. He shuddered. He would have to remember not to do any hugging if he could possibly help it.

A tall figure strode toward Dan out of the gloom. "You! Identify yourself!" it barked. Dan jumped in alarm. The figure was a SuperTough Army Dude soldier toy, dressed in a neat uniform and carrying a toy rifle, his sturdy plastic body rippling with muscles. Dan could not help but notice that the soldier had no head. Instead, a large foot protruded from his neck.

"Um, I'm Dan," said Dan. "Hi. I'm a Snugaliffic Cuddlestar."

"Dan, sir! Pleased to meet you, sir!" announced the soldier brightly, facing slightly to the left of where Dan was standing and holding out his hand for him to shake.

Dan waved. "I'm here. Can't you see me?"

The soldier shook its head (or rather the foot it had for a head) sadly. "Apologies, sir! My eyesight is not 100 percent effective due to a slight error during my manufacture. I have, as you may have noticed, a foot where my head should be."

Dan reached out his paw and shook his hand but the soldier quickly snatched it away. "Pleased to meet—"

"Yowch!" cried the soldier. "You have quite the grip, sir! You nearly took my hand off!"

"Sorry," said Dan. "I'm too strong. That's my problem. It's why I'm down here. I take it this is where they keep the faulty toys before they . . . ?" His voice trailed away.

The soldier nodded its foot. "Indeed, sir. But have no fear! You and I shall be out of here in no time!" He reached into his coat and produced a scroll of rolled-up paper tied with a blue ribbon. "Here, sir, is a map showing the secret exit to this dungeon! And at long last I have met someone with good enough eyesight to read it for me! Observe!" He untied the ribbon and spread out the map on the dusty floor.

It was then that Dan saw that it wasn't a map at all, but an old chocolate bar wrapper.

"Well?" asked the soldier excitedly. "Can you see the way out?"

"Um," said Dan awkwardly, "not really, no."

"Why not, sir?" demanded the soldier. "The plastic duck I acquired it from assured me it was the very best map available. I exchanged my entire knapsack and spare batteries for it! Surely it must tell us *something* of the local geography?"

"I think you've been conned, pal," said Dan.

A sudden booming growl filled the air, followed by the pounding of immense feet. Dan looked up, startled, and saw a huge shape advancing on them . . .

"What did you say, sir?" yelled the soldier above the rising din.

"Never mind!" called Dan. "Just run! Quick! Before it's too . . ."

A vast mechanical poodle was cantering toward them, its long ears flapping, its electronic eyes flashing vacantly, and its metal mouth gaping hungrily. Before Dan knew what was happening, the enormous dog had scooped up the soldier in its huge jaws and carried him off. Dan dived for cover behind a pile of old boxes and watched in horror as the dog's stumpy tail retreated, wagging, into the blackness and the soldier's cries faded away. Then, except for the constant low humming in the air, there was stillness and silence.

Dan blinked. How was he going to get out of this awful place? Surely there was something a bear of his strength could do? But what?

"Come with me," said a voice, interrupting his thoughts. It was low, female, urgent.

"What now?" said Dan, dazed.

A hand gripped him by the fur on his chest and pulled him into a tumbledown shack assembled from old-fashioned wooden building blocks. The interior of the shack was almost as dark as the outside, lit only by a single flickering candle.

"We'll be safe in here. For a while, anyway," said the voice. "Patsy the Poodle doesn't normally come sniffing around unless there are toys stupid enough to stand around in the open."

Dan rubbed his eyes with his paws and saw that the voice belonged to a rag doll. She was pale, with dark stringy pigtails and a pale pink heart on each cheek.

"What just happened?" he asked. His electronic heart was still thumping madly.

The rag doll gave a bitter laugh. "Welcome to the rejects pile, sweetheart. If the toy technicians don't shred you for spares, you can bet your life that one of the malfunctioning crazies down here will come after you sooner or later. It's a doll-eat-doll world out there. Which is why I'm leaving. And *you're* going to help me."

"Don't tell me," said Dan. "You've got a map."

The rag doll cackled. It was not the friendliest of sounds. "So you met the foot soldier, did you? Poor fool. No, I haven't got a map. What I have got is a *plan*." She suddenly grabbed Dan again by the fur on his chest and pulled him closer. "So—are you going to help me, or do I have to *make* you?" She raised a fist threateningly.

Dan raised his paws. "Whoa. I'll help. I want to get out of here as much as you do."

The rag doll considered this for a moment and then released him. "Sorry, furball. I'm not good with people. It's why I got dumped in here. Got a crossed wire in my brain that gives me a *really* short temper. The day I was bought I ended up dangling some little brat by the ankles out of her bedroom window because she looked at me the wrong way. Her parents didn't take too kindly to that, I can tell you. Man, I hate kids! Do you?"

Dan shrugged. "Haven't met any yet. Was looking forward to being bought and doing a bit of hugging, to be honest."

She grimaced. "Hugging? Yuck! Are you trying to make me puke? It isn't pretty when a Snaztacular Ultrafun toy pukes, believe me. Oil everywhere."

"I won't be able to hug anyone, though," Dan added sadly. "They made me too strong."

If Dan had hoped this remark might

provoke a little sympathy from the rag doll, he was disappointed. Instead, she cackled again and dug an elbow in his ribs. "I knew you were a tough guy right away, mister—but a teddy bear who's too strong to give you a hug? That's hilarious! Now I've heard everything!" She cackled again, but then when she saw Dan's hurt expression her face softened. "Ah, don't mind me, I'm just kidding. The name's Arabella, by the way."

"I'm Dan," said Dan. "Forgive me if I don't shake paws."

"Okay, listen up. The only way out of here is via *that* air vent up there." She pointed upward through a hole in the shack's roof at a tiny square of light high up on the ceiling. "The vent has iron bars across it. That's where you come in, muscles. You think you could bend those bad boys apart?"

Dan shrugged. "I'll give it a try. But how do we get up there?"

A crooked smile crossed Arabella's face. "Tell me, Dan. You ever play a game called 'One-Potato-Two-Potato'?"

They worked quickly, taking apart Arabella's shack and piling each block on top of the next until they had a rickety tower that almost reached the air vent. Dan teetered at the very top, stretching his arms as far as he could.

"How are we doing?" called Arabella from below.

"Almost there," replied Dan. "One more block and I think I'll be able to reach the bars."

"Well, bad luck, furball. That was the last one. Do you think you could reach the bars if you jumped?"

"Maybe. Maybe not."

From somewhere nearby came a hideous barking sound.

"Let's go with 'maybe,'" said Arabella. "And quick! That pain-in-the-neck poodle's got our scent, and she's heading straight for us!"

"What?" yelled Dan. The ground began to shake, and their building-block tower wobbled alarmingly. Below, he could hear the pounding of the huge dog's paws. It was getting closer.

"Hold on!" called Arabella. "I'm coming up!"

"Be quick! The dog's almost . . ."

There was a string of fearsome metallic yelps below them and then an ominous crashing sound. Arabella shimmied up the tower with lightning speed just as the mechanical dog smashed into its base. Building blocks began to rain down onto the floor.

"Jump, you stupid bag of fur!" she called up to Dan.

"Here goes!" Dan said, and leaped into the air. Something grabbed his foot. For a moment he thought the dog had caught him in its jaws, but then he realized it was Arabella hanging on to him. He stretched his arms as far as he could, fearing his seam might split and spill his electronic innards. But his seam held, and his two strong paws grasped firmly onto one of the iron bars of the vent. The two toys hung there for a moment—Dan from the bar and Arabella

from Dan's foot—breathless, while beneath them the giant poodle snapped and snarled. Dan peered down at Arabella. "You okay?"

"What are you waiting for, you furry lump? Christmas?" barked Arabella. "Get bending!"

CHAPTER THREE

A HARD RABBIT
TO BREAK

Dan had no trouble bending apart the iron bars of the air vent. He hauled himself and Arabella upward into the light. They emerged into a parking lot on the edge of a scrubby piece of woodland behind the Snaztacular Ultrafun factory. Above them, the morning sun blazed down from a perfect blue sky. Dan squinted upward. He had never seen the sun before. The heat from it felt nice on his fur.

Arabella dashed off into the trees without looking back. "Nice meeting you, mister. Thanks for taking care of those bars."

"Wait!" called Dan. "What happens now?"

"How should I know? You're a bear. Go and eat a marmalade sandwich or something." She disappeared into the undergrowth.

Dan glanced up at the sun briefly, as if checking that it was still there, and then hurried after her.

Arabella strode briskly through the trees, the sunlight dappling her pale face. She seemed to know where she was going.

Dan followed a few paces behind, trying to keep up. "Where can we go?" he asked. "We're toys who can't be around children. What sort of future is there for us?"

Arabella stopped and turned to face him. "You still here?"

"I'm serious," said Dan. "What do you think I should do?"

Arabella waved her arms. "Do whatever you want! Me, I heard there's an amusement arcade on the other side of these woods. I've worked out a system to beat the slot machines. Basically I'm going to beat them with my fists until the money comes out. Can't wait to try it."

"I couldn't do that," said Dan. "I'm not interested in money."

Arabella gave an exasperated sigh "Then don't! Don't you get it, furball? We can do anything we want. *Anything.* We're completely and utterly FREE!"

Somewhat ironically, it was at this moment that they both stepped into an enormous net, which suddenly hoisted them into the air. The two toys let out screams of fear and astonishment. They hung in the net, which rotated slowly like an enormous yo-yo hanging from a string, and pondered this strange turn that events had suddenly taken.

"Well, well, well . . . ," said a squeaky voice. "Looks like the spider just caught himself a couple of juicy flies!"

Dan and Arabella writhed and wriggled in the net to see who had spoken. It turned out not to be a spider at all, but a rabbit—what appeared to be a small, cute-looking fluffy rabbit doll wearing sunglasses and a rather formal white shirt and tie.

"Get us down from here!" yelled Dan.

"You heard the bear!" agreed Arabella. "Cut us loose, pronto!"

The rabbit folded its arms and chuckled. "Now why would I want to let a pair of thieves like you go free?"

"We're not thieves," said Dan. "We're toys. We just escaped from the factory."

The rabbit lifted its sunglasses and squinted at them through two tiny pink eyes.

"That's just what a pair of thieves *would* say, isn't it? Why are people always trying to steal from me, I wonder?"

"Oh *come* on!" said Arabella, losing patience. "We're not here to steal anything. Believe it or not, we have better things to do than skulk around in the woods robbing rabbits. What does a rabbit have that's worth stealing, anyway?"

"Oh, I've got lots of things worth stealing," said the rabbit.

"Like what?"

There was a long pause. Eventually the rabbit said, a bit feebly, "These sunglasses are quite expensive . . ."

"Sunglasses?" hooted Arabella. "Why on earth—"

A harsh robotic voice cut off her words.

"HALT! DO NOT MOVE!"

From the surrounding vegetation there emerged ten tall robots. They were roughly humanoid in shape but squarer and chunkier, as if made from some child's construction toy. These were policebots—robot law enforcement officers designed to be superior in every way to human police: unfeeling, unbribable, unstoppable.

"What's going on?" said Arabella, twisting inside the net to get a better view.

"Oh, *great!*" cried the rabbit sarcastically. "The policebots have been after me for a long time since I walked out on them. And you brought them right to me!"

"This is nothing to do with us!" cried Dan. "Honestly!"

"SILENCE!" screeched one of the policebots. **"THE PRISONERS WILL BE TAKEN IN FOR QUESTIONING."**

"Guess again, metalhead!" called the rabbit defiantly, dropping his sunglasses and springing onto the shoulders of the policebot who had spoken. He reached down a paw and swiftly unclipped the battery compartment

set into the policebot's back, reaching inside and ripping out the policebot's batteries. The policebot began to slump to the ground, powerless.

"FREEZE!" cried another of the policebots, raising its nightstick, but before it could react the rabbit had leaped onto *its* shoulders and yanked out its batteries, too. With breathtaking speed and agility, the rabbit bounded from the shoulders of policebot to policebot, removing the batteries from each until every robot sank to the ground, motionless.

The rabbit stood in the center of this ring of collapsed robot bodies, panting slightly, and gave a weird, high-pitched giggle of triumph.

"Wow!" said Dan. "That was incredible!"

The rabbit gave a modest shrug. "The Series 8 policebot is known for its dicey battery compartment. All I did was jiggle the magnetic clasp on the negative power coupling. Piece of cake, really."

Dan laughed. "If you say so, pal." Suddenly

there came an ear-splitting din of rotor blades. A sleek black helicopter swooped into view, hovering over their heads.

"What now?" muttered Arabella. "All I wanted to do was punch a few slot machines! I never asked for this craziness."

The helicopter emitted three loud cracks.

Three small metal disks flew through the air. One attached itself to Dan's arm, another to Arabella's arm. The third stuck squarely to the rabbit's forehead.

"What are these things?" asked Dan, trying to remove the disk and finding it was stuck fast. A great wave of tiredness suddenly washed over him.

"Electromagnetic pulse mines, by the look of them," said the rabbit. "Very latest technology. Releases a burst of energy that scrambles your brain for a few seconds. Makes you go unconscious."

As if to prove the point, he immediately fell over, unconscious.

CHAPTER FOUR

AUNTIE KNOWS BEST

Wood, thought Dan blearily as he came to. *I'm surrounded by wood.*

And so he was. As his head began to clear he saw that he was in a large office with wood-paneled walls. There was also a large wood-paneled desk, behind which sat a middle-aged woman with a sunny expression and a lot of curly yellow hair.

He tried to move but found he was strapped tightly to an ornate wooden chair. His muscles felt weak. Craning his neck, he saw that Arabella and the rabbit were beside him strapped to similar chairs.

"Nice of you to join us, furball," said Arabella.

"I don't suppose you know where we are or what on earth is going on or anything like that?" asked Dan hopefully.

"Not a clue, sweetheart," said Arabella brightly. "I'm just taking today one devastating shock at a time."

"Will you two imbeciles pipe down?" barked the rabbit. "I'm trying to concentrate on loosening my muscles so I can wriggle out of these restraints. There's a simple trick to it if you can just focus your mind . . ."

"Children! Children!" bellowed the woman behind the desk. Her voice was surprisingly loud and deep. "No one is going to be wriggling out of anything! Will all of you please just relax and button your lips for thirty seconds, and I'll explain what you're doing here."

"I know why I'm here!" growled the rabbit. "Because those stinking policebots—"

"Flax! Please shut *up*!" hissed the woman. "You know nothing of why you're here. Let me speak. Please."

The rabbit glowered at her but said nothing.

"Thank you," said the woman. "Firstly, let's

have some introductions so we know who's who. I've done a little research, and I've enjoyed learning all about you."

She tapped a button on a tiny laptop on her desk. A TV screen the size of a small swimming pool lowered itself gently down from the ceiling. Dan gaped at it. The woman gave him a wink. "We have all the latest technology."

On the screen were images of Dan, Arabella, and the rabbit, with various pieces of information written beneath each. The woman pushed her glasses farther up her nose and read aloud from the screen. "Dan is a Snugaliffic Cuddlestar teddy bear. He was made too strong. About a thousand times too strong, it seems. Arabella is a Loadsasmiles

Sunshine rag doll. She has the attitude of a bad-tempered rattlesnake. Despite his cuddly appearance, Flax the rabbit is not a toy at all, but a custom-made police robot disguised as a rabbit to dig tunnels and secretly gather information from criminals. He went AWOL some time ago and has been living wild ever since."

"I ran away for a reason!" declared Flax the rabbit. "A very good reason, I'll have you

know. Someone stole something from me. Something very important. And I'm trying to get it back."

The woman waved a hand, silencing him. "That is not my concern. All three of you are runaways. All three of you could quite legally be dumped in an incinerator or scavenged for spares."

"I'd like to see you try . . . ," growled Flax. "I'll bite your legs off!"

Arabella groaned. "Will you just zip it, big ears, and let the woman speak?"

Flax made a harrumphing sound but didn't say anything else.

"Thank you, Arabella," said the woman curtly. "My point is that you three misfits possess unique abilities. Dan, your strength.

Arabella, your . . . fighting spirit, shall we say? And Flax, your police experience. I'd like to offer you a job."

Flax's tiny pink eyes grew wide with surprise. "Me? Work for you? Are you out of your mind?"

"I have to say," said Arabella, "that while this bunny at my side may well be a few lettuce leaves short of a Caesar salad, I think he has a point. Why the heck would we want to work for you? We don't even know who you are!"

The woman smiled. "Very well. Here's some information, then. My code name is Auntie Roz. I work for the **DEPARTMENT OF SECRET AFFAIRS**. My job is to prevent horrible things from happening. The horrible blowy-uppy kind of things, for instance. Or the horrible 'Oh no, the gold at Fort Knox has been stolen!' kind of things. You get my drift? Now, let me tell you about a particular horrible thing I would like you to help me prevent."

She tapped a key on her laptop. The image on the screen disappeared and was replaced by two photographs. One showed a rather sullen-looking boy of about eight years old. He was wearing the uniform of some expensive private school.

Arabella's lip curled with disgust. "*Kids . . . ,*" she muttered. "*Yuck!*"

The second photograph showed a bizarre creature with the body of a human being and the head of an elephant. This strange human/elephant hybrid was dressed as a clown and wore a tiny conical hat decorated with a furry pom-pom. The creature was holding a box of breakfast cereal.

Dan shuddered. He could tell the elephant creature was trying to appear friendly, but to him it looked like something that had escaped from a nightmare.

Flax was very quiet. He studied the two images intently with his tiny pink eyes.

"The boy," said Auntie Roz, "is Sam Spinks, son of the senator Harry Spinks. Sam is shortly to end his school year and begin his six-week summer vacation in Maine. The elephant is—"

"He's called Rusty Flumptrunk," Flax interrupted. "I know all about the creep. That elephant and I have unfinished business."

"Indeed," said Auntie Roz. "Maybe you'd like to tell Dan and Arabella about him?"

Flax leaned forward as much as he was able to in his restraints. "He's the mascot for Wheatie Lumps breakfast cereal. *Was*, anyway. In the old days, a company mascot used to be an out-of-work actor in an animal costume.

Nowadays the companies genetically engineer mascots. Rusty is an artificial life-form, half human, half elephant. He was originally created to sell Petersen's Peanut Butter, but it turned out he had a peanut allergy—couldn't even smell one without getting sick—so they

sold him to the Wheatie Lumps Corporation. At first, he was a big success: kids loved him, and sales of Wheatie Lumps went through the roof. But then the Wheatie Lumps people began to work him too hard: every day more ads, more public appearances. It got to be too much, and in the end he snapped. Quit the job and formed an organization called the Army of Mascots, recruited lots of genetically engineered mascots from other big companies: Roxy the Cheese Leopard, the Baked Bean Elf, Hoopla the Shoe-Polish Crocodile. Loads more. They turned to crime, taking revenge on the corporations that exploited them, stealing anything they could get their hands on. I was part of the police team that finally put the Army of Mascots behind bars last year, but Rusty himself escaped at the last minute. Nasty piece of work, that elephant. Believe me."

"Thanks, Flax," said Auntie Roz. "Most informative. Here's the final piece of the puzzle. We've had word that Rusty Flumptrunk wants to kidnap Sam Spinks and hold him for ransom, with the aim of getting his Army of Mascots released from prison. The simplest thing would be to lock young Sam away

58

behind closed doors for his own safety until the threat is dealt with, but the senator doesn't agree. He wants his son to lead as normal a life as possible. Which is where you three beauties enter the picture."

"I don't understand," said Dan.

Arabella groaned. "Don't you get it, fuzzbrain? She wants us to be the kid's bodyguards. Am I right?"

Auntie Roz nodded. "Indeed. I want you three to work undercover, pretending to be Sam's toys. It will be your job to protect the boy from danger at all times. If Rusty Flumptrunk does try to snatch him, you will be ideally placed to prevent it."

"You seem to be forgetting one little thing, though," said Arabella.

Auntie Roz raised her eyebrows.

"I hate kids!" Arabella chuckled. "Dan here's so strong he'd probably cuddle the poor brat to death. And would you seriously let that loopy ex-police bunny near anyone's kids, let alone a senator's? I doubt it."

Auntie Roz smiled, as if she had been anticipating the question. "You won't have to actually *play* with Sam. He has real toys of his own. Your job is simply to look cute and guard him from danger so the boy doesn't need half a dozen six-foot security guards breathing down his neck all day. And we're hoping your unthreatening appearance may tempt the elephant into making a move so we can capture him. Can you do that?"

"I'm in," said Flax suddenly, decisively. "I accept the assignment."

Arabella frowned. "What's in it for us?"

"Other than not being junked and used for spare parts?" replied Auntie Roz with a smile. "You'll be rewarded. Richly. I promise."

Arabella screwed up her nose. "Don't have much choice, do I?"

Auntie Roz looked at Dan. The teddy bear had a thoughtful look on his face. "And what does our Snugaliffic Cuddlestar have to say?"

"I don't know if I can do it," said Dan quietly. "Arabella's right. I'm too dangerous to be around children."

"Nonsense!" said Auntie Roz. "Toy technicians may not be able to reprogram you, Dan, but you can reprogram yourself. You can learn to be more gentle if you really want to."

"Is that possible?" asked Dan.

"Anything is possible if you set your mind to it."

"Hey, don't spoil this for us, Dan," hissed Arabella. "Seems like only ten minutes ago you were complaining you had nothing to do."

Dan shrugged. "Okay. I'll try. But I'm not promising anything . . ."

"Splendid!" cried Auntie Roz, clapping her hands. "The name of this new team will be *Spy Toys*."

"But I'm not a toy," objected Flax "I'm a police—"

"Oh, just go with it, big ears," muttered Arabella. "I think it's a cool name."

Auntie Roz touched a key on her laptop, and the restraints binding them to their chairs retracted. She regarded her new recruits with an impish glint in her eye. "Okay, guys and dolls. If you're going to work for the **DEPARTMENT OF SECRET AFFAIRS**, I need to know you've got what it takes. Time, I think, for a little test."

"A test?" repeated Dan warily. "I'm not good at tests."

Auntie Roz winked. "Don't worry, little bear. This one'll be child's play."

CHAPTER FIVE

FUN AND GAMES

Auntie Roz ushered them into an elevator, along a gloomy passage, and out through a heavy steel door into the open air. The three Spy Toys found themselves on what appeared to be a bustling street in Washington, D.C. But, bizarrely, none of the people on the sidewalks or the cars and trucks on the road were actually moving. Everything was frozen in place, silent and motionless. Dan felt as if he had somehow stepped into an enormous photograph. He tapped the arm of an elderly lady standing nearby and realized she was made of wood.

"This mock-up of a street is where we train

our agents in combat," explained Auntie Roz. "You will face many dangers working for the **DEPARTMENT OF SECRET AFFAIRS**, and we need to know that you can look after yourselves."

Arabella snorted. "Don't you worry about that, sister. Furball here's as strong as an ox. I've seen the rabbit in action, and he's pretty hot stuff. And me?" She raised her fists and kissed both of them in turn. "I can look after myself."

Auntie Roz raised her eyebrows. "Perhaps. But we've discovered the toughest test a toy can ever face, and now . . . all three of you must face it."

The oil running through Dan's cogs and gears seemed suddenly to chill.

Flax folded his stubby little arms. "What you got? Army? Navy? Policebots? I'll take them all on."

Auntie Roz shook her head. "Something much worse." She raised a slender cell phone to her ear and spoke into it. "Our three new recruits are ready. You may release the McBiff Triplets."

"Who are the McBiff Triplets?" asked Dan.

"Toddlers," said Auntie Roz. "Two and a half years old. Bit of a handful, truth be told."

Arabella shuddered. "Kids? *Ugh.*"

"They don't sound all that scary to me," said Dan.

"Yes," agreed Flax. "What sort of challenge are three little brats going to be?"

The elevator doors slid open. The Spy Toys

turned to see three short, squat figures emerge. They were indeed toddlers—a boy and two girls—dressed in brightly colored outfits and carrying rattles, but there the resemblance to normal children ended. These toddlers had huge, powerful muscles like bodybuilders, horrible vicious expressions on their faces, and tiny ratlike eyes that glowed with malice. Each Triplet's name was written on the front of their romper in bright yellow letters: *Hayley, Duncan, Jacqui.*

"The McBiff Triplets are the children of a circus strongman and strongwoman," explained Auntie Roz. "They're much in demand to test army equipment and heavy industrial machinery. They test things *to destruction*, you see. No destructive force

has yet been found that's greater than a toddler. And these particular toddlers are the most destructive of all. Good luck." She retreated to a safe distance, cupped her hands to her mouth and called, "Hey, Triplets! Look at these nice new toys I've brought for you to play with!"

The McBiff Triplets fixed their mean little eyes on the Spy Toys—and then charged.

Dan gulped.

Before he knew what was happening, the Triplet named Hayloy was upon him, pulling his fur, twisting his limbs, biting painfully into his ear with her nippy little teeth. Dazed by the speed of this assault, he tried to bat the savage little girl away as gently as he could but, deftly avoiding his paws, she pushed him over backward, and he struck his head on a metal lamppost, which half stunned him.

"Ha ha!" guffawed Hayley. "Teddy falled over!"

Flax was faring no better. The Triplet named Duncan had him grasped by the neck and was thrashing him around wildly. The rabbit's eyes were rattling in his head like jelly beans in a jar.

The final Triplet, Jacqui, trotted up to Arabella and smiled a sweet gap-toothed smile. "Hello, Miss Rag Doll!" she said brightly. "Want to play a game?"

Arabella backed away nervously, raising her hands. "Um, er, no. I'm good, thanks," she mumbled. All her usual bravado seemed to have drained away.

"WELL I DO!" Jacqui screeched. She pounced on her like a lion on a wildebeest. Nearby was a wooden model of a mother pushing a baby carriage. Jacqui elbowed the mother aside, seized the baby carriage, and bundled Arabella inside it. "Ha! Now you're my baby!" she screeched. Arabella tried to clamber out, but Jacqui used the baby carriage's safety straps to tie her down. "Stay there! Naughty baby!"

"Hey!" called Arabella. "Furball? Bunny? Little help here?"

"Bit busy right now," said Flax, his voice wobbling as Duncan continued to thrash and whip him through the air. There was a loud popping noise, and Flax's head flew off and bounced down the road. "*Ah*," he muttered grimly as his head clattered to a halt against the curb. "This is not going terribly well."

"Hold on," said Dan. "I'll help you both." He tried to get up but none of his limbs would budge. *"Aw, no,"* he groaned. "A wire

must have come loose in my motor! I can't move!"

"Poor widdle teddy!" sniggered Hayley. She scooped Dan up and hugged him tightly to her. Dan grimaced, unable to move. Her

breath smelled of licorice. This was not how he'd imagined his first hug.

"What a dismal performance," said Auntie Roz, shaking her head. "I was obviously wrong about you three. Ah well, at least the McBiff Triplets will save us the bother of taking you apart for spares."

Crushed in Hayley's throttling embrace, Dan could just see from the corner of his eye a small gray shape nearby on the sidewalk. A wooden pigeon, obviously placed there by whomever had designed this mock-up of a city street to give it an extra touch of realism. All of a sudden, a great rush of thoughts tumbled through his brain. He tried to arrange them into a plan . . .

"Oh, look, kids!" he called in as friendly a voice as he was able to muster. "Look at that lovely pigeon on the sidewalk there. Isn't it nice? Shall we find some breadcrumbs to feed it?"

The McBiff Triplets swiveled their ratlike little eyes toward the pigeon. From their foul, leering expressions, Dan could tell that feeding it was the last thing on their minds. Like a pack of crazed hyenas, the three toddlers fell on the hapless wooden bird, thumping it, throwing it to one another like a ball, and kicking it savagely up the street.

"Flax!" hissed Dan. "Quickly! While they're distracted. Help Arabella, and then she can help me!"

"It may have escaped your attention, Dan," muttered Flax, "but my head's come off!"

"Then *use* it! And quick!"

Flax groaned, and, using his ears, he began

to haul his head slowly toward Arabella. When he reached the baby carriage, he began to throw his head against the wheels, making it wobble. One final throw caused the baby carriage to topple over. Then, speedily, Flax used his ears to untie Arabella's straps. The rag doll clambered out of the baby carriage and raced over to Dan.

"What do I do?"

"There's a small maintenance compartment set into my back," said Dan hurriedly. "Unclip it, and plug the loose wire back into my motor."

Arabella obeyed and instantly Dan felt the power surge back into his limbs. She then located Flax's body and quickly reattached his head.

"What a shambles," muttered the rabbit, rubbing his sore neck. "We can't even defeat a bunch of preschoolers. I pity the senator's child if he's got us protecting him."

"Maybe we'd have stood a better chance if you hadn't lost your head so quickly!" growled Arabella.

"I didn't notice you being much use," said Flax with a sniff. "What were you doing in that baby carriage? Waiting for a bedtime story?"

"Excuse me for interrupting, guys," said Dan through gritted teeth, "but there's still the small matter of these three maniac kids over there who want to tear us limb from limb."

"We need to trap them somehow," muttered Flax, thinking hard.

"That van!" said Arabella, pointing at a large vehicle nearby with the words **SHIFTALOT REMOVAL COMPANY** printed on its side. "We could lock them in the back."

"Nice idea!" said Dan. "I'll open it, and let's see if we can lure the Triplets inside." He raced over to the van and yanked on the handle of its rear door. There was a loud

CRAsSsSHHHH!

sound as the door was torn violently off its hinges. Dan stared dumbly at the buckled metal door in his paw.

"You furry buffoon!" yelled Flax. "You ripped the door off! That van's no good to us now!"

"Um, sorry, guys,"

said Dan sheepishly. "Don't know my own strength sometimes."

"We *know*," said Arabella with a roll of her eyes.

Hearing the commotion, the McBiff Triplets turned and stared at Dan and the others, their tiny eyes narrowing. Jacqui kicked the wooden pigeon into the gutter. "Toys!!!" yelled the three toddlers with insane delight and began to stampede toward them.

"Anyone got any more brilliant ideas?" asked Dan hopefully. "Because now would be the perfect time to speak up."

Flax's small pink eyes darted around frantically. "There's a wooden dog behind you, Dan. That might distract them like the pigeon did."

Dan spun around and saw a wooden model of a cheerful-looking sandy-colored Labrador. He grabbed it. Instantly, it shattered into tiny splinters. "Oh! Sorry! I tried really hard not to break it that time."

"I can't believe it!" moaned Flax. "He's done it again!"

"Good job, furbrain!" muttered Arabella, eyeing the approaching McBiff Triplets. "I hope you're ready to be trashed by these three little bundles of joy."

The terrible toddlers were almost upon them now. Dan turned his head away—and that's when he noticed the lamppost and got the idea. It wasn't a brilliant idea, as far as he could tell, but even a poor-quality idea is better than no idea at all, and he thought it worth a try.

As fast as his motorized limbs would propel him, he sprinted to the nearest lamppost and pulled it out of the ground as easily as a garden weed. Then he held it sideways like a tightrope walker's pole and ran at the McBiff Triplets.

"What's he doing?" asked Flax.

Arabella shrugged. "Beats the heck out of me."

The three children's eyes grew wide with surprise. They turned and began to run in the opposite direction, whimpering with fear.

Dan increased his speed. On reaching the Triplets, he bent the lamppost into a bow and used it to tie together the three thrashing, kicking infants.

"Careful with that lamppost now!" called

Auntie Roz from her vantage point. "If you squish those children, we'll have an extremely angry strongman and strongwoman on our hands, and nobody wants that."

Dan frowned, staring at his paws, willing them to obey his commands. Wincing with concentration, he pulled the lamppost bow as tight as he dared until the McBiff Triplets were fastened securely in its knot. They wriggled and whined but were perfectly unharmed.

"Waaaah!" bawled Hayley, kicking her legs uselessly. "Bad teddy!"

Dan slumped onto the sidewalk, exhausted.

"You did it!" cried Arabella. "Good going, furball!"

Auntie Roz began to applaud. "Indeed!

Well done, Dan. Perhaps you can control your strength after all, eh?"

"Perhaps I can!" said Dan. "If I concentrate really, *really* hard!" He laughed with pleasure.

Flax extended a paw to help Dan up. "Come on, bear. Let's get out of here."

Dan took the paw. There was a sound of crunching metal as Flax's arm came off.

CHAPTER SIX

THUNDER SOCCER

The huge twin-rotored helicopter touched down gently on the circular helipad. A hatch opened in its side, and three tiny figures emerged and dashed along a gravel driveway toward an imposing country house. It was

early evening; the sun was low, and it made
the three figures cast long spindly shadows
in the shapes of a teddy bear, a rag doll, and
a rabbit.

A uniformed security guard was waiting for them. He opened the sturdy front door of the house and ushered them inside.

★ ★ ★

They were led to a large, warm study filled with bookshelves and comfortable old furniture. Sitting on a pair of elegant leather chairs were a man wearing a neat suit and a bored-looking boy of about eight, who was slumped with his arms crossed, aimlessly kicking his heels.

The man rose to his feet in welcome. "Good evening," he said in a voice dripping with well-educated charm. "I'm Harry Spinks. This is my son, Sam. I understand you'll be taking care of Sam during his summer vacation here."

The boy peered at the Spy Toys uncertainly. "One of them's a rag doll? They're *girls'* toys."

Before anyone could reply, Arabella had grabbed Sam by the collar and was pinning him to the floor. "Listen, pipsqueak!" she growled. "Let me teach you a lesson about something called *gender stereotypes*. There's no problem at all with boys playing with dolls, and don't let anyone tell you differently. In fact—"

She didn't get any further because at this point several security guards stormed into the room and dragged her, still ranting, off the unfortunate child. Sam sat up, dazed, and began to whimper.

Flax shook his head and covered his eyes with a paw. "What a start," he muttered.

"I'm so sorry about this," interjected Dan hurriedly, seeing the appalled expression on the senator's face. "Our colleague Arabella here is a bit nervous because she knows how important an assignment this is for us. I'm sure she'll be able to keep her enthusiasm in check from now on." He stared pointedly at

Arabella, who returned his gaze fiercely but then got the message.

"Oh, right, yeah," said Arabella. "The senator's kid. Sorry, everyone. My bad. No hard feelings, eh, Sam?" She smiled winningly at Sam, but the boy squeaked and dived behind his father.

"I'm not convinced that this is such a good idea," murmured the senator. He gave his son a nudge. "Come out from there, boy. Don't be a coward."

Tentatively, Sam peeped around his father's back. "I'm not a coward," he muttered glumly. "That rag doll caught me by surprise, that's all."

"I assure you, sir," piped up Flax, fiddling nervously with his tie, "that we are all highly skilled security operatives. You can rely on us to be professional at all times. I guarantee it."

The senator nodded at the security guards, and they released Arabella. He regarded the three Spy Toys uncertainly. "Well, which would you prefer?" he asked his son. "Being permanently accompanied by a gang of burly security guards all summer?

Or hanging out with these *three*..." He
paused, unable to find a suitable noun. "With
these three. Well?"

Sam looked at the Spy Toys. Arabella smiled
cheerfully and gave the boy a thumbs-up
sign. Flax straightened his tie and grinned,
somewhat cheesily. Dan raised his eyebrows
hopefully.

"I'll give them a try, I suppose," said Sam,
without much eagerness.

"Excellent!" said the senator. "Guys, you're
hired!"

★ ★ ★

Not long afterward, Sam was kicking a
soccer ball around an enormous lawn beside
the parking lot at the back of the house. The
soccer ball, being a product of the Snaztacular

Ultrafun Corporation, was returning promptly to Sam's foot after every kick.

Dan, Arabella, and Flax spread out along the edge of the lawn and began slowly to patrol its perimeter. The air was pleasantly warm, and small insects darted amid the flowers. The three Spy Toys kept in touch with one another via tiny walkie-talkie headsets, although it was Flax who seemed to be doing most of the actual talking.

"Six fifty-one p.m.," announced the rabbit into his headset, checking his wristwatch. "No sign of any sinister elephants."

"Oh *really*?" replied Arabella. "That's exactly what you said at six fifty, six forty-nine, six forty-eight, *and* six forty-seven!"

"No need for that attitude," said Flax stiffly.

"I'm simply being thorough about the important job we have to do."

"You're being *boring*, is what you're being!" said Arabella. "I don't need your squeaky little voice in my ear every sixty seconds telling me everything's fine. Here's an idea. A sinister elephant shows up—you yell out, 'Hey, everyone! There's a sinister elephant!' Until then, why not keep your carrot hole closed?"

"Uh, look, guys," said Dan with a note of weariness. "We're supposed to be a team, remember? We should all make the effort to be friends."

"What do you want me to do—hug him?" snarled Arabella. "I told you—hugging makes me puke."

"You don't have to hug him! All we need to do is *get along* with one another."

"I'll happily get along with that brain-dead bunny as soon as he eases off on the constant status updates."

"Insults now, is it?" said Flax. He tutted. "I might have guessed. This is what I get for working with amateurs."

"Now wait a minute, hare-brain . . ."

"Hey, everyone!" yelled Flax with sudden urgency. "There's a sinister elephant! There's a sinister elephant!"

"What?" cried Arabella.

"Where is it?" said Dan. His eyes automatically went to Sam. The boy was engrossed in his game and seemed fine.

"Oh, hang on," said Flax. "My mistake. It's a watering can."

"A watering can?" repeated Dan, confused.

"How in the world can anyone mistake a watering can for a sinister elephant?" hooted Arabella. "Are you blind?"

"It caught me off guard," said Flax, a little defensively. "Lurking there in the shadows by that bush. I panicked."

"And *you're* the professional one?" sniggered Arabella. "The tough ex-cop bunny gets spooked by a piece of gardening equipment! Piece of free advice, pal. Don't ever look inside a shed. You'd pee yourself."

"Well, it was a very sinister-looking watering can," said Flax.

"You're an idiot!"

"No. I think you'll find it's you who is the idiot, Arabella."

"No, you're the biggest id—"

Dan switched off his headset. The silence was delicious.

"Hey!" called a voice. "Hey, you! Teddy bear!"

Dan looked around. It was Sam. He was gesturing for Dan to come to him. Obediently, Dan trotted over. The boy was bouncing the soccer ball on the neatly mowed grass.

"Yep?"

"Play with me," said Sam.

"Can't, I'm afraid," said Dan. "I've got a job to do."

"Oh, pleeeeeease," said Sam, making big puppy-dog eyes. "I never have any fun when I'm at home."

Dan raised his eyebrows. "Are you not having fun playing soccer now?"

Sam shook his head glumly. "No. I hate soccer! But Dad loves it, and he makes me practice all the time. He even bought me a professional standard Snaztacular Ultrafun ball to boss me around. If it doesn't think I'm trying hard enough, it gets all sarcastic and starts making fun of me. Come on. It'll be more fun if you play! Those other two are keeping watch. You can join in for five minutes."

"What's that, Sam?" asked the soccer ball in a bossy tone. "Stop mumbling and start kicking! Or is the little weed too tired to play anymore? Does he want to snuggle his teddy instead like a little baby? Ha!"

Dan smiled politely at Sam. "One moment." He reactivated his headset. "Listen, guys . . ."

"What is it?" asked Flax. "Has the child spotted any sinister elephants?"

"No," said Dan. "No elephants. He just wants me to play soccer with him for five minutes."

"What? This is most irregular."

"Do you think that's a good idea?" asked Arabella.

"I think so," said Dan. "We should get to know the boy if we're going to be protecting him. We have to learn to be around children, don't we?"

"Whatever you say, Dan," said the rag doll. "Just be careful."

Dan turned to Sam. "Right. We're on. What do you want to play?"

"Oh, nothing complicated," said Sam. "Just

some pickup soccer. I pass to you, you pass to me?"

"No problem."

"Great!" Sam ran to the far end of the lawn, dribbling the soccer ball as he went.

"Get a move on, boy!" said the ball loudly. "Put some effort into it for once, you lazy little toad!"

Sam gave the soccer ball a good whack with his foot, and it shot across the lawn toward Dan. Dan readied himself. He would just give the soccer ball the tiniest possible kick. The weakest little tap.

"Oh dear. Now the teddy's going to kick me," called the soccer ball mockingly as it sped toward him. "Ooooh, I'm *soooo* scared. Soft toys are nothing more than cushions with eyes sewn on them, if you ask me. I bet—"

BAMMMM!

The sound of Dan's foot connecting with the ball was like a thunderclap. The soccer ball flew screaming through the air, fast as a missile, missing Sam's head by inches, actually ruffling his hair as it passed over him, and

slammed into the side of a long silvery car in the parking lot. There was a huge

BANGGGGG!

as the car exploded in a shower of broken glass and fragments of twisted metal. Alarms began to blare. Shouting voices could be heard inside the house.

Dan stood frozen with terror, his mouth hanging open, as he surveyed the damage he had caused.

"I believe the word you're looking for, Dan," said Arabella's voice in his headset, "is *whoops*."

★ ★ ★

"I ought to have you stuffed with sawdust and shoved in a case in the Natural History Museum with a sign attached saying *Ursus idiotus.*"

"Huh?" said Dan, frowning.

"What I'm trying to say is that you're the stupidest bear in the whole wide world, Dan. Do you understand me?"

"Oh," said Dan. "Um, yes."

He was in the senator's study, talking to Auntie Roz on the computer. The image of Auntie Roz on the monitor may have been small and flat, but from the noise it was making and from the terrified look on Dan's face, you would have thought there was an angry tiger in the room with him. He shuffled uncomfortably, trying to meet Auntie Roz's gaze and failing.

Sam and his father were also there,
listening in to the scolding. The senator's
expression was grim.

"Not only do you nearly kill the child you
were supposed to be protecting," continued

Auntie Roz, "you destroy the senator's priceless antique Rolls-Royce. You're amazing, Dan! You're a one-bear disaster area! I thought you could control your strength!"

Dan winced. "So did I."

"It doesn't matter about the car," said the senator. "Sam's safety is all that concerns me."

"Looks like we'll have to take you off the assignment, Dan," said Auntie Roz. "Sorry. But we can't risk any more of these foul-ups."

Dan nodded. It was a silly idea anyway, he thought, expecting a reject like him to make a suitable bodyguard for a child.

"It wasn't Dan's fault," said Sam with sudden decisiveness. "I made him play soccer. I didn't know he was super-strong.

If anyone should get in trouble, it should be me."

Auntie Roz frowned. "Is this true?"

"Yes," said Sam. "Let me keep the bear! Please?"

Auntie Roz considered. "Hmmm. What do you think, Senator?"

The senator scratched his chin thoughtfully. He fixed the teddy bear with a serious gaze. "Dan—can you guarantee my son will come to no harm in your care?"

Dan met his eye. "All I can guarantee is that I'll try my very, very best. That may not be good enough. But it's all I've got." He shrugged.

The senator nodded. "Very well. I admire your honesty, Dan." He turned to the screen.

"You may continue with the current operation, Roz. Good evening." He strode briskly from the room. Sam winked at Dan and then trotted after his father.

Auntie Roz fixed Dan with a steely look.

"The first time we met, Dan, I said we use the very latest technology here in the **DEPARTMENT OF SECRET AFFAIRS**. *You* are one of those pieces of technology—and right now you're acting like faulty merchandise."

"But I *am* faulty!" protested Dan.

Auntie Roz silenced him with a wave of the hand. "You've shown before that you can control your strength. *So do it*. Or back to the factory you go."

CHAPTER SEVEN

THE ICE CREAM CAPER

A few nights later, Dan took his turn standing guard in Sam's bedroom while the boy slept. Flax and Arabella sat slumped in a corner with some of Sam's other playthings. Snaztacular Ultrafun toys had their own version of sleep in which they reverted to their lowest power settings overnight to conserve energy, and the rag doll was snoozing away contentedly. Flax, while not a toy, had a similar feature for preserving battery power, and he was dozing fitfully beside her, occasionally emitting the odd

quiet squeak as he dreamed whatever it is that robotic ex-police rabbits dream about.

The room was still and silent, lit only by a shaft of silvery moonlight peeking in through a crack in the curtains. After the troubled start to their assignment, Dan enjoyed these quiet sessions of late-night sentry duty, glad to be away from the grown-up humans who always seemed to be telling him off.

He heard a sharp gasp. Suddenly, Sam turned on his bedroom light and sat up, rubbing his eyes.

"You okay?" asked Dan. His eyes darted around the room. Had the boy heard some suspicious sound that he had missed? An intruder prying open the window, perhaps?

Or an unfamiliar footfall outside the door? He adopted a crouching, ready-for-action pose.

"Had a nightmare," said Sam. "Dreamed a giant frog was trying to steal my soccer shoes." He shivered. "It was *horrible*."

"Oh," said Dan. "Sorry to hear that." Had Dan been a normal Snugaliffic Cuddlestar bear, he would have offered Sam a nice hug at this point, but Dan knew that a hug from him was the last thing anybody needed. "I could bring you some warm milk?"

Sam shook his head sadly. "No, thanks. The only thing that cheers me up after I've had a nightmare is ice cream."

"Want me to get some?"

"I'm only allowed to have it once a week as a treat—and I've had this week's share already." He heaved a mighty sigh.

Dan laughed gently. "I'm sure nobody would mind if you had a bit more ice cream. Especially after a nightmare."

"You mustn't tell anyone I had a nightmare!"

117

said Sam, suddenly panicked. "Especially not Dad! He'll only call me a coward again and embarrass me."

"Don't worry," said Dan, heading for the door. "I won't tell anyone."

"Wait!" called Sam. "There are security guards everywhere. If they see you taking ice cream they'll know it's for me, and Dad'll find out."

Dan gave a shrug. "So I'll steal some. Go on a commando raid."

Sam's eyes widened. "Really?"

"Why not?" Dan padded over to the window and slid it open. A chill night breeze crept into the room. "I bet I can climb across the roof and let myself in through the kitchen skylight. Be in and out in thirty seconds!"

"That sounds like amazing fun! Let me come with you!"

Dan sniggered. "Yeah, right! Can you imagine what would happen if your dad found out I let you sneak across a rooftop? He'd have me taken apart and thrown in a Dumpster! No, young man. You are staying right here."

"Then let me give you something to help you," said Sam. He opened a toy box and began rummaging inside. "Where is it?" he muttered. "I know it's definitely—*aha!*" He brought out what looked like a long, thin snake wrapped in transparent plastic.

Dan eyed the thing warily. "Not poisonous, is it?"

Sam chuckled. "It's not a snake. *It's a jump rope!* A Snaztacular Ultrafun one. Dad bought it for me when he wanted me to take up boxing. Apparently boxers have to jump rope a lot to stay fit. Never thought about trying it but you can use it to lower yourself into the kitchen. It extends to any length you need." He ripped the plastic wrapper off it and pressed the activation button on one of the rope's handles.

"Hi there!" said the rope in a jaunty voice. "I am a Snaztacular Ultrafun Jumptastic Jumpmaster Play Rope! I have been programmed with over three thousand beloved children's jump rope rhymes. Here's one of my favorites!" And now the rope began to sing loudly:

"I know something,
but I won't tell.
Three little monkeys,
in a peanut shell.
One can read,
and one can dance,
and one has a hole,
in the seat of his pants!"

"Will you be quiet?" hissed Dan. "You'll wake up the entire house!"

"Sorry!" said the rope brightly. "It's just that I love singing almost as much as I love jumping!"

Sam giggled. "Okay, listen up, rope," he said, feeling slightly foolish because this was

the first time he had ever given orders to a piece of rope. "I want you to obey Dan the teddy bear here and help him in his mission. Do you understand?"

"Sure thing!" said the rope. "I love teddy bears!" And once more it began to sing:

> "Teddy bear, teddy bear,
> turn around.
> Teddy bear, teddy bear,
> touch the ground.
> Teddy bear, teddy bear,
> show your shoe.
> Teddy bear, teddy bear—"

"Shut up, you stupid rope!" pleaded Sam. "We don't need you to sing. At all! Got that? This is a top-secret mission, and no one can see or hear you!"

"Sure!" said the rope. "Not a problem!"

Sam coiled up the rope and handed it to Dan. "Good luck."

"Thanks." Dan looped the rope over one shoulder like a mountaineer and stepped through the open window. "Any particular flavor?"

"Chocolate," said Sam. "Every time."

Dan winked. "You got it."

With slow, careful steps, Dan crept along the narrow ledge that skirted the exterior of the house between the first and second stories. On the grounds of the house below, he saw the occasional beam of a security guard's flashlight as he carried out his

nightly patrol. Rounding a corner, he saw
beneath him in the moonlight the rectangular
outline of the kitchen wing—an old stable

building that had been refurbished and connected to the main house. The large square skylight set into its flat roof was open.

Much of the outside of the old house was covered with thick fronds of ivy. Dan tested one to see if it would take his weight and then climbed down. He padded soundlessly along the roof of the kitchen and peered through the skylight. He and the other Spy Toys had been given a tour of the whole house on arrival, and he knew that there was a tall freezer almost directly beneath where he was standing. There was also, he remembered, a security guard stationed right outside the kitchen door.

"Jump rope?" he whispered to the rope over his shoulder.

126

"Yup?" answered the rope in a loud voice.

"You have to keep your voice down!" hissed Dan. "Remember?"

"Oh, yes! Sorry!" said the rope quietly.

"I want you to tie one end of yourself securely around that chimney *there*, and then tie the other end of yourself around my waist. Got that?"

"Got it!" the rope whispered cheerfully and obeyed, swiftly knotting itself around first a chimney and then Dan's tummy.

Dan tested the knot. It was secure "Okay," he whispered. "You're going to lower me down into the kitchen. I'll wave my paw once when I want you to stop lowering, and if I wave twice I want you to hoist me back up. Understand?"

"One hundred percent!" said the rope. "Ready when you are!"

"Right."

With a final glance down at the grounds to check for security guards, Dan clambered through the skylight, and the jump rope began to lower him gently into the kitchen. It was eerily quiet; the surfaces of every appliance and every hanging pot and pan were coverd in a film of silvery moonlight. After a few feet, the jump rope suddenly stopped the descent without warning.

"What's wrong?" whispered Dan.

"A thought occurs," said the jump rope.

"I'm not interested in the thoughts of a stupid jump rope," hissed Dan. "I've got a mission to carry out. Can we save the

philosophizing for when we're back in Sam's room?"

"It's just," continued the rope a little nervously, "if you open the freezer door, the light will come on, and the security guard outside might notice."

"Ah," said Dan. "Good point, actually. Yes. Thanks for bringing that to my attention. What do you suggest?"

"There's a switch on the back of the freezer. There on the wall. Switch it off, and the light won't come on."

"Brilliant!" whispered Dan. "Let's do that!"

The rope lowered Dan down a little farther until he could reach the power button. He switched it to "off." Then the rope lowered him some more until he was level with the handle of the freezer door. Using the tiniest claw on his paw, Dan eased the door open.

There within lay the prize they sought.
Row upon row of tubs of ice cream.
Strawberrylicious Creamigoo, Carameltastic

Fudgesquelch, Coconutty Fatslurp . . . Dan grinned and removed a tub of Chocko-wonderful Squishyum. "I was obviously wrong about you," he whispered to the rope. "You're a genius! Sam's going to be tickled pink when he sees this ice cream!"

"Ice cream!" yelled the jump rope, and began to sing loudly:

"Ice cream sundae, lemonade, punch,
Spell the initials of your honeybunch!
A, B, C, D—"

"Will you be quiet, you idiot!" hissed Dan. "They'll hear us!"

The kitchen door burst open, and a powerful flashlight beam swept the room.

"Oops, sorry!" whispered the rope. "I couldn't help it."

"Take me up!" hissed Dan at the rope. "Now!"

"I thought you were going to wave your hand twice when you wanted to go up?" said the rope.

"No time!" said Dan, and he grabbed at the rope, attempting to shinny up it and escape.

"You shouldn't have pulled so hard!" said the rope. "My other end's come untied!"

"What? Aaagh!"

In an instant, Dan and the rope plummeted to the kitchen floor in a painful heap.

"Who's there?" called the security guard.

Dan dropped the tub of ice cream, and he and the rope dived for cover under the white

table cloth that hung down to the floor from the large kitchen table. They froze and listened breathlessly as the sound of the security guard's footsteps grew steadily louder . . .

Suddenly, the guard's radio crackled. "All units," said a voice, "report to greenhouse in rear garden immediately. Repeat: all units report to greenhouse immediately!"

The guard made an impatient tutting sound, turned on his heel, and stalked from the room.

Dan and the jump rope slid out from under the table, breathing sighs of relief.

"I wonder what happened to the greenhouse?" said Dan.

"Oh, I just threw my soccer ball at it," said

a voice from above. "I thought it might distract them."

Dan looked up and saw a smiling face peering through the skylight.

"Hurry up with that ice cream," called down Sam. "My tummy's rumbling!"

CHAPTER EIGHT

SNOW WAY OUT

Dan swished down the mountainside in a graceful arc, his skis bringing him to a gentle stop at the bottom of the slope. Below him, a series of farther slopes fell away to the valley floor like an immense white staircase. Despite the lingering warmth of late summer, the snow was crisp and glittered like an ocean of tiny jewels. In fact, it wouldn't have mattered how hot it was—there would still have been snow because the whole mountain had been covered with Snaztacular Ultrafun Nevermelt Permasnow.

"Fancy moves, furball," said Arabella approvingly. She and Sam were waiting for him.

"Hang on," said Dan. "We're missing someone. As usual."

Sam giggled and pointed up the slope. "I think this is Flax now."

A large snowball was rolling down the mountainside. Jutting out of it was a pair of long white ears . . .

Nearly a month and a half had passed since the Spy Toys had taken up their assignment as Sam's bodyguards. In that time Dan and his two colleagues had carried out their duties without a hitch. There had been no plots to kidnap Sam, no dangers against which to protect him. The long summer vacation was drawing to a close, and in a matter of days Sam would be back at his boarding school. After his initial doubts about whether he was up to the job, Dan realized he actually quite enjoyed being a Spy Toy.

Today, they were skiing at the mountain resort a few miles away from the senator's country house. Sam loved to ski and had decided to teach the Spy Toys so that they could accompany him. Arabella had taken to skiing instantly. Dan had eventually mastered the art after several attempts, responding quickly to Sam's patient, good-humored instruction. But Flax had never got the hang of it and skied with all the grace of a bag of melons.

The snowball tumbled and bounced down the slope and came to rest near a clump of bushes.

"Don't worry, pal," said Dan brightly, as he, Arabella, and Sam dashed over to help. "I was awful, too, when I first started. Bit more practice is all you need."

Digging into the snow, Sam suddenly gasped. He held up two long strips of white fabric. "Look!"

"You stupid bunny," growled Arabella. "You snapped your ears off!"

"I don't think these are Flax's ears," muttered Sam, examining the fabric.

"Then what are they?" asked Dan.

Arabella clawed the snow from Flax's body. "Have you put on weight, bunny? And you look all gray! That can't be healthy!"

Dan's electronic heart pounded. "Get back, everyone! That's not—"

Before he could finish speaking, a tall, powerfully built humanoid elephant exploded from the remains of the snowball.

Arabella's mouth flopped open in surprise. "Rusty Flumptrunk!"

"Sorry I can't stick **aroooound!**" trumpeted the elephant in a loud voice, his

two white tusks gleaming. "But it's time for this elephant to

FLYYYYY!"

He snatched up Sam in his powerful arms and threw the boy in the back of a sleek sledlike snowmobile he had hidden in the nearby bushes, then bounded into the driver's seat. The snowmobile's engines roared into life, and the vehicle sped off down the mountainside in a cloud of blue-gray smoke.

"Playtime's over, furball," said Arabella grimly. She and Dan dug their ski poles into the snow and hurled themselves down the slope.

The two toys zoomed down the snowy mountain, trees whizzing past and the wind whipping their faces. They could see Rusty Flumptrunk's snowmobile in the distance, clouds of snow spraying in its wake. The vehicle executed a dramatic skid, almost overbalancing, and shot off in a different direction.

"Where do you think he's going?" asked Dan, shouting to be heard above the wind.

Arabella pointed. "See that wooden bridge over the valley? Believe he's heading for that. It's the quickest way back down to the town."

"I bet I can catch them if I use all my strength," said Dan. He bent his knees, preparing to spring forward.

"Hold up, mister," said Arabella. "Let's use our heads. It'd be much easier if you threw a boulder at the bridge and smashed it. That would cut off his escape."

Dan squinted into the distance. "But there's a bunch of children crossing the bridge!"

Arabella shrugged. "Yeah, but they're not the *senator*'s children, are they? No one would miss them *that* much."

Dan grinned and shook his head. "I think I prefer my way."

He thrust his ski poles into the snow and launched himself forward with the speed of a

145

rocket. Teeth clenched, eyes narrowed, he streaked down the slope, gaining quickly on the snowmobile as it veered and swerved.

Faster . . .

Faster . . .

He could smell the snowmobile's acrid exhaust fumes, hear the elephant's trumpeting laugh, see Sam clinging desperately to his seat in the back of the vehicle . . .

They neared the bridge. A few children were still crossing. They screamed and scattered as the snowmobile tore its way over the flimsy wooden structure. Rusty Flumptrunk shot out his trunk and gave the floor of the bridge a vicious thump. The wooden planks fell away into the snowy abyss as the whole bridge began to collapse. In an instant, the bridge was nothing more than splintered pieces of wood plummeting toward the valley floor. The snowmobile zoomed safely onto the opposite side of the valley and raced off into the distance.

But it was too late for Dan to stop himself. He tried desperately to reduce his speed and fell, his skis snapping and sending him tumbling headlong toward the cavernous drop down the cliff face into the valley. He clawed at the ground, gouging great grooves in the earth with his paws, but nothing could prevent him from sliding toward the edge. Eventually the solid ground beneath him seemed to vanish, and he was falling . . .

. . . falling . . .

. . . but only until he grabbed hold of a thick tree root jutting from the face of the cliff. He hung from the root, angry with himself for not being quick enough, and wondered how he would ever get back up. The growl of the snowmobile's engine receded into the distance, and with it went his last scrap of hope of rescuing Sam.

A thick tree branch lowered itself into his view. Dan blinked at it.

"Grab onto this, furball," called Arabella's voice from the top of the cliff. "And if you accidentally pull me down and we both end up falling to our deaths, you and me are gonna have serious words."

★ ★ ★

Dan and Arabella made their way down the mountain as quickly as they could. They found the snowmobile abandoned on the little road that led to the town.

"I wish Flax were here," muttered Dan as they examined the snowmobile for clues. "He'd know how to track that elephant with his police training. I wonder what happened to him."

Arabella shrugged. "Never thought I'd say this, but I sort of miss that crazy bunny. Still, we've got a job to do, Dan. We can't wait. Finding Sam is our priority."

Dan nodded grimly. "Yep. I know."

"Hey!" said Arabella brightly. "What do we have here?" She held up an empty burger carton. Dan noticed that the floor of the snowmobile was littered with them.

"So he likes burgers? So what?"

Arabella raised her eyebrows. She held out the empty carton for Dan to see. "Look at the slogan."

Dan read the words embossed on the top of the carton:

CHOMP-A-LONG BURGERS & FRIES
14 MAIN STREET
BiG ENOUGH TO FEED AN ELEPHANT!

CHAPTER NINE

THE ELEPHANT IN THE ROOM

The large square building rang with chatter. It was a busy morning at the **CHOMP-A-LONG BURGERS & FRIES** restaurant, and its manager, a young woman named Delia Sparrow, was endeavoring to keep her customers happy, her staff polite and efficient, and her food as unhealthy as possible. People loved the fact that **CHOMP-A-LONG BURGERS** didn't pretend their products were good for you, unlike so many of the other fast-food companies. There was no vegetarian option. Everything was deep-fried in a rich, gooey kind of cooking fat, including the salad and the actual burger buns themselves. The bosses at **CHOMP-A-LONG** headquarters liked to joke that the reason no one ever complained about their products was that once you'd eaten a **CHOMP-A-LONG BURGER**, you were so bloated and sluggish that you couldn't even pick up a phone.

Delia wiped the sweat from her brow with a forearm. She had been working extra hard for the past few days because an inspector from headquarters had been visiting. Not that this inspector seemed to have done much actual inspecting. He was named Mr. McTembo and had remained locked away in a back room, presumably writing a report on the restaurant, venturing out only occasionally to go for jaunts on his snowmobile. Mr. McTembo had worn a long overcoat with an upturned collar and a large fedora hat pulled down over his face. He kept in touch with Delia from the office via an intercom system, although all he ever seemed to do was demand in a loud trumpeting voice that food be left outside his door.

The restaurant staff had their hands full this morning with a party of children who had been staying at the nearby ski resort. Skiing, it seemed, was hungry work, and the children were wolfing down their burgers and fries as fast as Delia and her staff could serve them. There seemed to be a mysterious shortage of mayonnaise, too. Every last container of the stuff had vanished overnight.

"Hello!" cried a voice cheerfully. Delia looked around in confusion. There didn't seem to be anyone there. But then she peered over the counter and saw two small toys standing at the front of the line: a teddy bear and a rag doll.

"Hi there!" cried the rag doll cheerfully, and Delia realized that they must be Snaztacular Ultrafun products, the sort of playthings who could walk and talk by themselves.

"Hello!" said the teddy bear. "We're government health inspectors here to carry out an inspection. You know the sort of thing— checking that the grills are at the right temperature and the fries are sufficiently greasy . . ."

Delia frowned. "But there's already an inspection going on. From headquarters."

"Er, yes, we're working with them," interjected the rag doll quickly.

"Don't mind us!" cried the teddy bear. "You won't know we're here!"

The two toys began to whisper to each

other and point at the various doorways that led off the main restaurant area.

"Just one moment, if you please," said Delia. She went to the wall and activated the intercom device. "Excuse me? Mr. McTembo? There are two toys here to take part in the inspection. A teddy bear and a rag doll. Do you know anything about this?"

"**Whaaaat?** Are you having a **laaaauugh?**" boomed a loud voice from the intercom. "Those toys have **noooothing** to do with me! Seize the little monsters and bring them to me **immmmmmmediately!**"

"As you wish, Mr. McTembo," said Delia. She clicked off the intercom and smiled slyly. "Excuse me, everyone!" she called to the throng of customers. "You see those toys over there? The teddy and the rag doll?" She pointed a finger at Dan and Arabella, who were creeping along the opposite wall. "The first person to bring me those toys will receive free food from this restaurant for a month!"

The children gave a great cheer and swarmed toward Dan and Arabella, arms outstretched, laughing wildly.

"We're cornered," said Dan, his back to the wall as the great stampede of children approached, threatening to engulf them. "What do we do?"

"I'll hospitalize the lot of 'em!" snarled Arabella, balling her fists.

"Don't be ridiculous," hissed Dan. "We can't fight kids!"

"Then what, fuzzbrain?"

"Wait," said Dan. "Give me your tights."

"They won't look good on you. Your legs are too hairy."

"I'm serious! Quickly!"

Arabella speedily removed her tights and

handed them to Dan. Dan swung them around in a loop, lassoing a light fixture high on the ceiling. He yanked hard on the stretchy material while Arabella grabbed his arm, and he and the rag doll were swiftly catapulted into the air at tremendous speed. Beneath

them, the tidal wave of children groaned with disappointment, their tiny hands clawing at the air. The two toys clung to the light fixture. Dan punched a hole in the flimsy ceiling, and he and Arabella climbed through into the dark, dusty space above.

"By my calculations," whispered Arabella as they crawled along on their hands/paws and knees, "we should be directly above the back office . . . now." She levered up a ceiling tile a tiny amount and squinted through. "Yikes, Dan!" she whispered. "There he is! The big ugly elephant dude himself! We need to work out a plan."

"Oh, I've got a plan," said Dan cheerfully. He made a fist. "It involves hitting things very hard indeed . . ."

POWWWW!

Dan pummeled his fists into the ceiling, which gave way instantly. He and Arabella tumbled down into the room below. They landed nimbly on their feet and took in their surroundings: a plain office containing a single wide desk, behind which sat the hideous, leering figure of Rusty Flumptrunk. His overcoat and fedora had been discarded, and he was clad once more in his customary clown suit and furry pom-pommed hat.

The elephant emitted a blood-curdling chuckle. "Well, bless **myyyyyyyy** tusks!" he boomed. "If it isn't the kid's **paaaaaaathetic** little robot bodyguards! How nice of you—"

"Wait!" said Arabella, holding up a hand. "You weren't actually going to say 'How nice of you to drop in,' were you?"

Rusty Flumptrunk coughed uncomfortably. "Maybe," he muttered.

Arabella groaned. "That line is so *old!*"

Dan nodded. "It's not exactly original, is it?"

"Enoooooough!" cried Rusty Flumptrunk, slamming his hand on his desk. "You two bozos didn't fall through my ceiling today just to criticize my comedy material, did you?"

"That's right," said Dan pleasantly, leaping onto Rusty Flumptrunk's desk and grabbing the elephant by the bow tie of his outfit. "We came here to rescue Sam Spinks. And if you like having your big head attached to your shoulders, you'll tell us *exactly* where we can find him."

"Take it **eeeeeeeasy**, little bear," snorted Rusty Flumptrunk with a sinister giggle, wriggling with surprising strength out of Dan's grip. "The kid's **fiiiiiiiine!** In fact, young Sammy's helping me with my fantaaaastic plan! See?" Using his trunk, he wrenched open the door to a closet.

Arabella and Dan let out twin gasps of astonishment. Inside the closet they saw Sam, gagged, his arms and legs bound, a terrified look in his eyes. He was tied to a large sinister-looking metal device.

A bomb.

And on it was a digital clock slowly counting down the seconds from five minutes to zero . . .

"The Mayonnaise Bomb!" announced Rusty Flumptrunk. "Forgive me **bloooowing** my own trumpet, but this plan is **SOOOO** clever! Either the senator orders the release of my Army of Mascots from jail, or young Samuel here and everything else within a fifty-mile radius ends up drenched in fresh mayonnaise! All machinery will seize up! Cars and buses will skid into one another! People's clothes, houses, and all their stuff will be rendered permanently yucky!" He thrust a cell phone at Dan with his trunk. "Call the senator now and inform him of the situation."

"You're nuts," said Dan simply. "Let Sam go and deactivate the bomb or—"

"Or **whaaaaaaaat?**" laughed

Rusty Flumptrunk. "You'll snuggle me to death?"

"Not a bad idea, actually," said Dan, advancing on him, fists raised.

"Sorry, my furry friend," snorted Rusty Flumptrunk, "but I can't stick around for cuddles. Bye **nooooooow!**" He suddenly sucked the cell phone up his trunk and then fired it at Dan with the force of a missile. The phone struck Dan squarely in the forehead, and he toppled over backward, unconscious. Then Rusty Flumptrunk grabbed Arabella by her collar and dashed out of the door.

"Let go of me, you enormous idiot!" screamed Arabella, kicking and twisting and biting and doing everything she could to escape from the elephant's grip. But it was no good.

"Sorry, my **deeeear,**" chuckled Rusty Flumptrunk. "You're my backup hostage. Always pays to carry a spare, eh?" He shoved open a fire exit at the end of a corridor and stepped out into the parking lot, heading for a large unmarked white van: his getaway vehicle.

"Not if I can help it, trunkface!" cried Arabella, and flung one of her long pigtails around Rusty Flumptrunk's legs. The elephant crashed heavily to the ground with a grunt of frustration. Arabella leaped onto his chest and planted a fist between his eyes. Rusty Flumptrunk groaned, and his enormous head slumped backward.

"I hope you like punches," grinned Arabella.

"Because I've got oodles more where that came from."

But then Rusty Flumptrunk let out a terrifying bellow of rage. His trunk shot out like a snake and gripped Arabella by the neck . . .

★ ★ ★

Dan opened his eyes, bleary, and shook his head. The clock on the Mayonnaise Bomb showed there were less than three minutes to go. He struggled to his feet and began to undo Sam's restraints.

"Don't waste time untying me!" cried Sam

once his gag was removed. "You need to defuse the bomb before we end up covered in mayonnaise."

"But I don't know how to do that!" said Dan.

"Use Rusty Flumptrunk's phone! Look up 'bomb defusing' on the Internet!"

"But I'm too strong! What if I accidentally set it off?"

"You have to do it!" said Sam. "Time's running out. Come on, Dan! You *can* do this! I believe in you!"

Dan picked up the phone . . .

★ ★ ★

Out in the parking lot, Arabella struggled in the grip of the elephant's trunk. Rusty Flumptrunk grinned evilly, preparing to slam her against the wall.

"Time for dolly to go bye-bye!" he chuckled.

★ ★ ★

Frowning hard, Dan stared at the screen of the phone. He had opened a small hatch in the side of the bomb. According to **howtodefuseacondimentbomb.org**, his task seemed simple enough. All he had to do was swap the blue and green wires. And not disturb any of the bomb's other workings. That bit was important.

Dan groaned. Why him? A faulty teddy bear who could barely control the power of his own super-strong muscles? Surely he was the last candidate anyone would pick to defuse a bomb. Wasn't he just a useless reject who should have been junked long ago? He winced at the thought of how he'd ripped a van's door off its hinges when trying to subdue the McBiff Triplets, and how he'd smashed up the senator's antique Rolls-Royce. But then he remembered how he had also expertly bent a lamppost and used it to tie the Triplets up in a neat knot. He thought about how he'd delicately opened the freezer door to steal some ice cream for Sam. He *could* do this.

With every scrap of concentration he could muster, he reached out his paw toward the blue wire. The only sound he could hear was the continual *click, click, click* as the clock counted down the seconds. He suddenly became aware of every cog and motor and electric circuit inside him. He could sense the electricity flowing through him, keeping him alive—and in that moment he could feel himself take control of every single muscle in his body. Every tiny motor that worked every limb and joint was his to command. He grasped the wire firmly, keeping his arm as still as possible, and tugged . . .

CHAPTER TEN

A BEGINNING,
A CUDDLE,
AND AN END

There was a sudden rumbling sound in the parking lot. A small heap of brown earth appeared on a little grass shoulder beside where Rusty Flumptrunk was preparing to slam Arabella against the wall of the restaurant. The earth shook and wobbled, and

a small white head with two long white ears suddenly popped out. "Flax!" cried Arabella.

"You!" cried Rusty Flumptrunk, staring in wide-eyed astonishment at Flax. He dropped Arabella in surprise.

"Long time no see, big nose," muttered Flax, his small pink eyes trained on Rusty Flumptrunk.

Arabella noticed Flax was holding a small tube. "What's that? A peashooter?"

Flax smiled. "A pea*nut*-shooter, actually." He dropped a single peanut into the tube and then raised it to his lips.

"Peanuuuuuuuuts?" cried the elephant in alarm.

"Of course!" Arabella said, grinning. "Rusty Flumptrunk's allergic to peanuts!"

FLLLOₒOOOPH!

Flax's aim was true. The peanut shot through the air, straight into Rusty Flumptrunk's mouth. Instantly, the elephant moaned and clutched his stomach. **"Oooooogggggh!"** he spluttered, sinking to his knees and turning blue, which is never a good color for an elephant.

Flax produced a pair of handcuffs and slapped them around Rusty Flumptrunk's wrists. "Oh, and one last thing," he said, kneeling down in front of the sick creature. The elephant stared back at him through bloodshot eyes. "They say elephants never forget, but rabbits have pretty good memories, too. You stole something from me, sir. The last time we met. Is this ringing a bell?"

Rusty Flumptrunk nodded guiltily. "Yes. Sorry, little guy. I—"

Flax waved a paw, silencing him. "And now at last I get it back."

He reached out and peeled the round fluffy pom-pom from Rusty Flumptrunk's conical clown hat.

Arabella frowned. "He stole a pom-pom from you?"

"This is no pom-pom," said Flax. "This is my *tail*."

"Your tail???"

Flax fitted his tail into its accustomed place on his rear end and gave it a couple of experimental wiggles. "Ah!" he cried in delight. "Good to have it back!"

Rusty Flumptrunk gave a sudden bitter laugh. **"Enjooooy** it while you can, bunny boy!"

Flax frowned. "Excuse me?"

"Oh my good gosh!" cried Arabella. "I forgot! The bomb!"

★ ★ ★

Arabella raced back to Rusty Flumptrunk's office to find Dan hunched over the bomb. In his paws he held the blue and green wires. On his face was a pained expression.

"Do you want me to do it?" she called. "I have a steadier hand!"

"Too late," said Dan, nodding at the clock timer. Its digital countdown was less than ten seconds from zero. "Seems it's up to me to hold the mayo."

"Good luck, furball!"

In one smooth, controlled movement, Dan placed the blue wire in the green wire's socket and the green wire in the blue wire's socket.

Instantly, the clock stopped ticking, its readout frozen at 00:00:02.

Dan turned to Arabella and shrugged. "One second to go would have been cooler, but I'll settle for that. Seems Roz was right. And Sam. I can reprogram myself to control my strength."

Arabella cackled delightedly. "Good work, mister!"

The door flew open, and a group of children burst in. "There they are!" cried one of them, still eager to take Delia up on her offer of free food. They advanced on Dan and Arabella, threatening to swarm them again.

"Hold them off for a minute while I untie Sam," hissed Dan.

"Me?" said Arabella. "But I hate kids!"

"Just try!"

For the next couple of minutes, Arabella kept the children distracted by entertaining them with jokes and acrobatics.

Soon the children were giggling helplessly at her antics. *Weird!* she thought as she

pretended to slip on an imaginary banana peel. *Who'd have thought making children laugh could be so much fun?*

Dan finally released Sam. The child looked unhurt, but his face was red, and there were tears in his eyes. He looked about as miserable as it is possible for an eight-year-old boy to look. "I was so scared," he muttered. "Dad was right. I am a coward."

"Don't be ridiculous," said Dan. "If you hadn't kept your cool and had that super-smart idea to look up bomb defusing on the Internet, we'd all be in the mayonnaise right now. And what about the time you rescued me and that crazy jump rope from the security guards? That took real courage. You're a hero, pal. High five!" He raised his paw, and Sam returned the high five with a satisfying slap. "Yowch!" laughed Dan, rubbing his palm. "That hurt."

Sam beamed at Dan and began to giggle.

★ ★ ★

The next day, the Spy Toys were called to an urgent meeting at the senator's office. There they found the senator, Harry Spinks, sitting behind his large wooden desk. At either side of him stood Auntie Roz and Sam. Both were wearing solemn expressions.

"Good afternoon," said the senator in a grave voice. "I have called you here today for a very serious purpose." He stared at them intently for a second and then broke into a wide grin and laughed. "Who wants some medals?"

The three toys exchanged shocked glances and then started to laugh, too.

The senator produced a shiny metal case and took from it three glittering medals on ribbons, which he placed in turn around the necks of Dan, Arabella, and Flax. "These," he said, "are to say thank-you for protecting my son and helping catch that awful elephant. You have been without doubt the bravest and most resourceful toys a child could have."

"And we're very proud to have you working in the **DEPARTMENT OF SECRET AFFAIRS**," said Auntie Roz.

The toys chorused their thank-yous and admired one another's medals.

"And finally," said the senator, "I have one more medal here. And it goes to my son, Sam, for his extreme bravery in the face of danger." He placed the medal around Sam's neck. "I'm very proud of you, son." He and Sam shook hands warmly, and Sam beamed with the purest pleasure.

"Enough of the mushy talk," said Arabella. "You trying to make me puke? Do we get money, too?"

Auntie Roz chuckled. "We have quite a reward lined up for you three. Don't you worry."

Arabella nodded appreciatively. "Cool."

Flax twiddled his tie. "Sorry about her. Anger issues."

Arabella raised a fist. "Say I've got anger issues again, Mr. Bunny, and I'll punch your buck teeth down your throat."

"See, that's just the sort of thing I'm talking about, Arabella . . ."

Sam touched Dan's arm. "Hey, you."

"Hi!" said Dan. "Nice medal!"

"I wanted to ask you something," said Sam. He bit his lip nervously.

"Go for it."

Sam took a deep breath, his eyes wide and moist. "Will you be my bear, Dan? My teddy bear? You can come back with me to my school when the school year starts again. Having you around for the past few weeks has been awesome."

Dan's jaw hung open and wobbled. After a short time he realized he must look ridiculous and ought to say something or close it. Eventually he managed to stammer, "Oh. Oh, wow. Sam, pal. That's. Oh. Wow. Gosh."

"So what do you think?"

Dan looked at the boy. He had a strange feeling in the circuits in his tummy and wondered if something inside him was broken. Wasn't this what he had always wanted? Why wasn't he jumping at the chance to be a real teddy bear? "The thing is, Sam," he said, "when they told me I could never be a child's toy, I didn't know what I was going to do. For a while I had no purpose, but now I do. And I've realized there's lots of things I'm good at and some things that only a super-strong teddy can do. I'm a Spy Toy, Sam. That's where I belong."

Sam gave a small, sad smile and nodded. "I understand. Can I at least have a hug?"

"A hug?" Dan scratched his head. He realized he had never actually given a hug to a real human being before, even though that was the very reason he had been built in the first place. "Are you sure?"

"I totally trust you not to squish me," laughed Sam, "if that's what you're worried about!"

Dan laughed, too. "Yeah, why not?" He opened his arms and gave Sam one of the nicest, friendliest, snuggliest hugs a Snugaliffc Cuddlestar teddy bear can give.

This joyous moment was spoiled only very slightly a moment later by the sound of Arabella being sick.

EPILOGUE

THREE MONTHS LATER

The toyshop at 115 Mulbarton Street looked shabby compared to the smart city businesses that were its neighbors. Cobwebs clustered in the corners of its grimy windows, and paint flaked from its battered wooden door, upon which a tattered paper sign that seemed permanently to announce **"BACK IN 10 MINUTES"** was crudely taped. The few old toys arranged haphazardly in its window display were sun-faded and laughably old-fashioned. Had you seen the place while out on a walk, you would have briefly wondered

how such a run-down store could survive in the center of the city, and continued on your way.

Inside, however, in the gloom at the back of this dingy shop, behind rows of dingy shelves stacked with dingy toys, stood a small, dingy door. Behind this door, which was surprisingly strong and secure for something so dingy-looking, lay something rather unexpected—the headquarters of Spy Toys, the newest team in the **DEPARTMENT OF SECRET AFFAIRS**.

Arabella slotted the CD into the player and slipped the headphones over her ears.

"Welcome," said a voice, "to lesson one of the Control Your Anger course . . ."

She closed her eyes.

She was in the living room of their luxurious apartment. Flax the rabbit was watching a documentary about interrogation techniques on a huge flat-screen TV. Dan was sitting at a table trying to build a house of playing cards, a look of fierce concentration on his face. The cards had been a present from Sam.

The telephone rang. He flinched, and the half-built house of cards collapsed, each playing card complaining in a loud voice (for they were a product of the Snaztacular Ultrafun Corporation).

Arabella ripped off her headphones with an annoyed grunt. "Cut the racket!" she bawled at the top of her voice. "Can't you see I'm trying to relax?"

Flax hurriedly answered the phone. He

listened for a moment and then pressed a button. "She wants to go on speakerphone."

"Hello, my darlings!" said the loud voice of Auntie Roz. "How are you finding your new digs? As you might expect from the **DEPARTMENT OF SECRET AFFAIRS**, the apartment's been fitted out with all the latest technology."

"Not bad," replied Flax. "Better than a hole in the ground."

"Good," said Auntie Roz. "Afraid I'm going to have to drag you away, though. Something has come up. An assignment. Rather a fiendish and dangerous one, as it happens."

Arabella groaned. "Do we have to?" She yawned. "We like it here! What if we don't want to go off and do dangerous things?"

Dan snickered quietly. It was true. The past few weeks they'd spent in their new apartment had been most enjoyable.

With a mechanical whir, three hatches opened in the ceiling and three large metal claws descended, each grabbing onto a Spy Toy and hoisting them upward. They howled in protest, legs kicking uselessly.

"Oh yes," chuckled Auntie Roz. "All the latest technology. Off we go on our new mission, then!"

Dan thought about using his super strength to free himself from the claw's grip, but realized with a sudden burst of happiness that he didn't want to.

MARK POWERS has been making up ridiculous stories since elementary school and is slightly shocked to find that people now pay him to do it. As a child he always daydreamed that his teddy bear went off on top-secret missions when he was at school, so a team of toys recruited as spies seemed like a great idea for a story. He grew up in north Wales and now lives in Manchester. His favorite animals are the binturong, the aye-aye, and the dodo.

★ ★ ★

TIM WESSON was born somewhere in England. As a young boy he enjoyed climbing trees and drawing pictures of dogs in cars. Eventually he became an illustrator who creates children's books. Tim doodles and paints whenever he can and likes to draw the first thing that pops into his head. He lives by the sea in Suffolk with his family.